THE GREATEST ADVENTURES IN THE WORLD

Jason
AND THE
VOYAGE TO THE EDGE
OF THE WORLD

TONY BRADMAN & TONY ROSS

ORCHARD

ORCHARD BOOKS

The text was first published in Great Britain in a gift collection called
The Orchard Book of Swords, Sorcerers and Superheroes with full colour illustrations by
Tony Ross, in 2003
This edition first published in hardback in 2004
First paperback publication in 2005

3 5 7 9 10 8 6 4 2

A CIP catalogue record for this book is available from the British Library.

ISBN 978 1 84362 472 1

Printed and bound in Germany by GGP Media GmbH, Poessneck

The paper and board used in this book are made from wood from responsible sources

Orchard Books
An imprint of Hachette Children's Group
Part of The Watts Publishing Group Limited
Carmelite House, 50 Victoria Embankment, London EC4Y 0DZ

An Hachette UK Company
www.hachette.co.uk
www.hachettechildrens.co.uk

CONTENTS

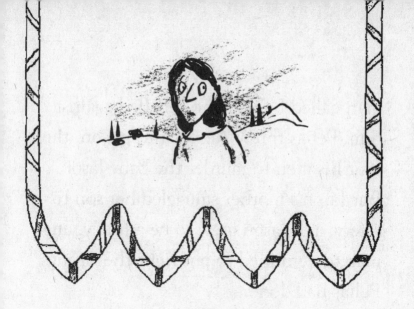

CHAPTER ONE
THE GOLDEN FLEECE

FOR A BOY FROM A ROYAL family, Jason had a pretty tough start in life. He was born a prince, the son of Aeson, the king of a Greek city. Aeson, however, had a brother, an evil, cunning man called Pelias, who rebelled against him. Pelias threw Aeson into prison, then sent his men to murder the baby Jason. But Jason's mother smuggled her son to safety, and Jason grew to be a fine young man, determined to put right the wrongs Pelias had done.

So, one day, Jason set
out for his home
city. As soon as he
arrived there, he
went straight to
the royal palace
and demanded
a meeting with
his uncle.

The guards took
Jason to Pelias, who
sat on the throne he had
stolen from Jason's father.

"How nice to see you, Nephew," Pelias
said. "Although somehow I have a feeling
you're not just here for a family visit.
What can I do for you?"

"You can free my father and give him back his kingdom," said Jason, proudly. "And if you do it now, I will ask him to spare your miserable life."

"Brave words," said Pelias, laughing. "I could have you killed on the spot – but wait, I've got a better idea. I'll do what you want...on one condition."

"Name it," said Jason quickly. "I hereby swear I'll accept whatever it is."

"Very well," said Pelias, grinning at his guards. "I will gladly free your father and make him king again – if you bring me the Golden Fleece."

The guards howled with laughter, and Jason realised he'd been tricked. It was an impossible task. Many had gone in search of the Golden Fleece, and none had returned. But Jason had sworn, and wouldn't go back on his word.

"Is that all, Uncle?" he said. "I was expecting something much harder."

Then he strode from the palace, the guards' jeering ringing in his ears.

But Jason was a lot less confident than he'd sounded. He wasn't even sure where the Golden Fleece was, although legend said it was across the sea.

So Jason went to Argus, the best shipbuilder in Greece, and asked for his help.

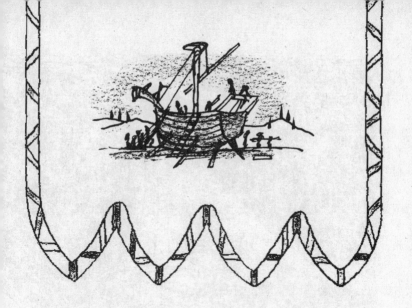

CHAPTER TWO
KING PHINEAS'S CURSE

ARGUS BUILT JASON A beautiful ship with a tall mast and fifty oars, and Jason called it the Argo. Then Jason let it be known he was going on a voyage of adventure, and needed a

crew of heroes to accompany him. They
came from far and wide, the greatest
warriors of their time. They called
themselves the Argonauts – which is
Greek for 'the crew of the Argo' – and
soon set sail. They travelled far, and saw
many wonders. They survived storms

and treacherous seas, they passed safely through the famous Clashing Rocks, they fought savage tribes and monsters, and they grew to be more than just the crew of a ship – they became a true band of brothers. And Jason asked everyone they encountered where the Golden Fleece might be found.

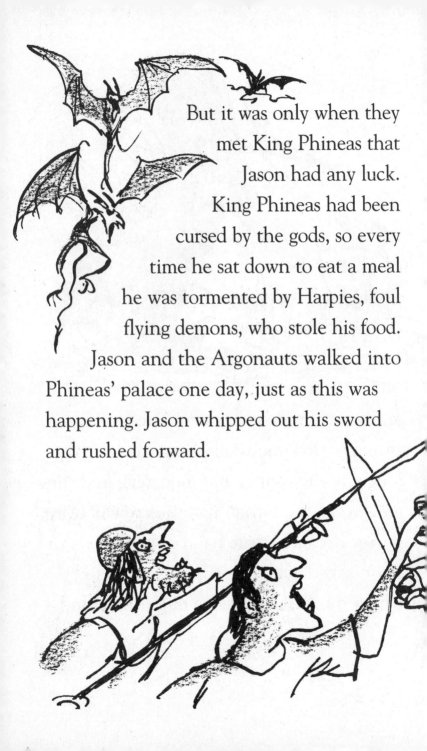

But it was only when they
met King Phineas that
Jason had any luck.
King Phineas had been
cursed by the gods, so every
time he sat down to eat a meal
he was tormented by Harpies, foul
flying demons, who stole his food.
Jason and the Argonauts walked into
Phineas' palace one day, just as this was
happening. Jason whipped out his sword
and rushed forward.

"With me, men!" he yelled, and a furious battle began.

The air was filled with terrifying shrieks as Jason and his men threw their spears, and slashed at the Harpies with their swords, or shot them down with arrows. And the Harpies fought back, beating at the Argonauts with huge wings and raking the men's shields and helmets with razor-sharp claws.

But the Argonauts won in the end, killing most of the Harpies and driving off the remainder. Phineas was overjoyed, and couldn't thank Jason enough.

"There must be something I can do for you in return!" Phineas said at last.

"You could tell us where to find the Golden Fleece," Jason said, putting his sword back in its sheath. "If you know, that is. Nobody seems to."

"I do know," said Phineas, the blood draining from his face. "But I wish you'd asked me anything else. To seek the Golden Fleece is certain death."

"The only thing that's certain," said Jason, "is that I must fulfil my quest."

Phineas was even more impressed
by Jason now. So he told him that the
Golden Fleece belonged to King Aeetes
of Colchis, and how to get there.

It turned out that Colchis wasn't far from Phineas's kingdom. So Jason and the Argonauts bade Phineas farewell, and a few days later they rowed into the harbour at Colchis.

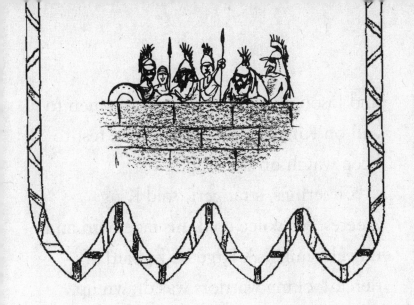

CHAPTER THREE

CRUEL KING AEETES

COLCHIS WAS A GRIM, forbidding city beneath an iron-grey sky. Soldiers lined the harbour walls, silently watching the Argo approach. The Argonauts tied up at the quayside, and Jason went with some of his men to call on King Aeetes, leaving the rest to keep watch on the ship.

"Greetings, stranger," said King Aeetes, his voice cold, his face hard and unwelcoming. A large bodyguard of fierce-looking warriors was drawn up behind his throne. "Perhaps you would like to tell us what brings you here."

"I've come to ask for your Golden Fleece," Jason replied, deciding it was best to be honest. He noticed there were some other people looking on from behind the bodyguards, among them a dark-eyed young girl who was staring intently at him.

"I need it to free my father and restore his kingdom," he said.

"Now why am I not surprised?" Aeetes muttered, giving Jason a thin smile.

"You're not the first young hero who's come seeking my Fleece, and I'll tell you what I've told all the others…it's yours, my boy. I will gladly hand it over to you – so long as you perform a couple of small tasks for me first."

"And what might those be?" Jason asked, warily.

"Why, nothing too difficult," Aeetes replied, giving Jason a brief flash of his cold, thin smile again. "Just a bit of ploughing, and sowing some seeds."

Jason felt sure Aeetes was plotting something, but he decided to go along with it for the time being. So he agreed, and Aeetes said he could perform the tasks the next day. Then he invited Jason and all his men to a great feast.

Jason sat next to Aeetes, but noticed the dark-eyed girl staring at him once more. He found out her name was Medea, and that she was the king's daughter. And he also discovered that he couldn't help staring at her, too.

At last the feast was over, and Jason and his men rose from the table to return to the Argo. But as Jason left the palace, someone tugged at his arm.

It was Medea, and she signalled for him to follow her to a dark corner.

"Here, you'll need this tomorrow," she

whispered, handing him a small jar of
ointment. "Be sure to smear yourself with
it before you start ploughing. Then listen
out for me to tell you what to do once
you've sown the seeds."

"But why do I need this?" Jason asked.
"And why are you helping me?"

Medea just kissed him, then slipped away. She loved her father, but as soon as she had seen Jason, she knew she loved him more. Jason thought it was all very strange, but he had fallen in love with her too. So, in the morning, he covered himself with the ointment before he and his men set off for the palace.

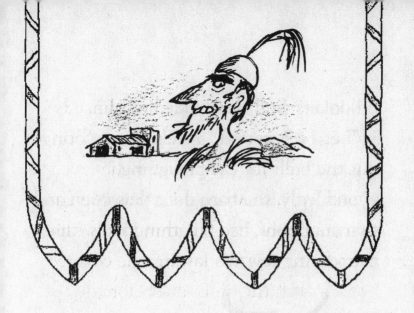

CHAPTER FOUR
JASON'S TASKS

AEETES WAS WAITING WITH his bodyguard at the gates, and led Jason and his men to a field nearby. There was a large barn to one side.

Jason spotted Medea among the other

onlookers, and she nodded to him.

"Let's get started," Aeetes said. "Bring out the bulls for the ploughing."

Suddenly, the barn door flew open and two enormous, fire-breathing bulls came thundering towards Jason.

But Medea's ointment protected him from their scorching flames. He got the bulls harnessed, and ploughed the field.

The Argonauts cheered their leader, but Aeetes frowned at Jason.

"The job's not done yet," said Aeetes. "Here are the seeds to sow."

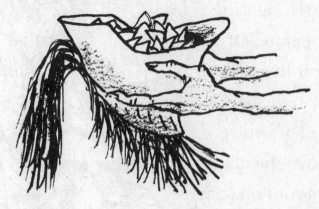

Aeetes gave Jason a helmet full of what looked like sharp teeth. Jason shrugged, and walked up and down the furrows he'd ploughed, casting the teeth to right and left. Little did he know that they were dragon's teeth.

To his horror, from each tooth
there sprang a fully-armed
man. Soon Jason and his
men were in a pitched
battle, fighting
desperately to save
their lives. Then
Jason heard
Medea's voice
above the clang
of sword on shield.

"Throw the helmet
at them!" she yelled.
"The one the seeds
came in!"

Jason did what he was
told – and the instant the helmet

landed amongst the warriors, they
turned on each other. Within
minutes they were all dead.
"I've performed the tasks
you set me," Jason said
angrily, striding up
to Aeetes. "Now
keep your part
of the bargain
– give me the
Golden Fleece."
"Of course," said
Aeetes, and smiled.
"You'll find it
in my garden."
Jason told his men to wait
while he went into the palace garden.

It was a strange, dark, overgrown place with an evil atmosphere. Jason shivered, and nearly jumped out of his skin, when Medea suddenly appeared beside him.

"Sssh…" she hissed at him. "We must be careful not to wake the dragon."

Medea led Jason to the heart of the garden, where a tall oak tree stood. Jason stopped in his tracks, filled with wonder – for there, hanging from one of the tree's branches, was the Golden Fleece. It shone with a magical glow, and was even more amazing than Jason had ever imagined it would be. He could hardly believe that this fabulous prize – something so many other men had died seeking – was at long last almost within his grasp.

But a huge dragon was curled before the tree, and Jason realised now why Aeetes had smiled – Aeetes thought Jason would never get past the Fleece's guardian. However, Medea had given the creature a drug to make it sleep.

Jason crept up and pulled down the Fleece. But the branch snapped as he did so, and fell across the dragon's scaly snout. Jason backed away, holding the Fleece – and his breath. The dragon slowly opened one eye, then the other. It looked at Jason…then leapt to its feet, roaring with fury.

"Run, Medea!" Jason yelled. He drew his sword and slashed at the great beast as it reared above him, then he turned and ran out of the garden too.

Aeetes was puzzled when he saw his daughter running past him – and furious when he saw Jason appear with the Fleece tucked under his arm.

"Kill the strangers!" Aeetes cried, and his bodyguard moved forward.

But just then the dragon burst out of the garden, roaring and breathing fire and stamping on anyone in its way. The palace and many of the nearby houses went up in flames. Aeetes's men panicked, and Jason saw his chance.

"Quick, men!" he called out above the din. "Back to the Argo!"

And so the Argonauts made their escape. Soon they were rowing away from Colchis as fast as they could, a tall, black cloud of smoke rising behind them. Medea stood close by Jason in the stern, knowing she would probably never see her father again. But she had made her choice, and she was happy.

Jason was happy too. He held the shimmering Fleece in his hands and smiled. He had Medea with him, and the Argonauts, his band of brothers. He couldn't wait to get back, to free his father and banish Pelias forever.

The Argo moved swiftly homewards over the dark sea, towards the setting sun.

JASON
ONE BOY AGAINST
THE WORLD

BY TONY BRADMAN

People have always been fascinated by the legend of Jason and his quest for the Golden Fleece. It's easy to see the attraction. There's plenty of adventure in the story – a voyage to strange, exotic places, encounters with monstrous creatures, a fabulous treasure waiting to be won. But it's Jason who is at the heart of the tale's appeal – or more precisely, the situation Jason finds himself in.

In ancient Greece, the story of Jason and his voyage was considered to be almost as important as the great tales of the Trojan War. Therefore, there were many poems and plays written about him, but the most famous version was *The Voyage of The Argo* by Apollonius of Rhodes, written in the third century BC.

Jason is a young boy deprived of his birthright, but determined to regain what is truly his. He has to face huge obstacles – the power and hatred of one king,

46

the lies and tricks of another, a perilous voyage to the edge of the world – and he does so with courage (and the help of some friends).

Folk tales, myths and legends from all over the world tell the stories of seemingly powerless characters who must overcome enormous problems to find their happy endings. The Persian tale of Ali Baba, for example, is about a poor man treated badly by his rich brother and threatened by strong, violent men. But Ali Baba survives, and they don't.

Another good example is the story of Joseph in the Hebrew Old Testament. Joseph is sold into slavery by his brothers and is taken to Egypt where he faces death. But eventually he becomes one of the most powerful men in the land.

We all have challenges to face, and sometimes they can seem very big, while we feel very small. But Jason's story seems to say to us that if he can succeed in his quest, if a powerless boy can take on the world and win, then we can be the heroes of our own lives too, whatever our problems.

No wonder it's a story people want to experience again and again.

THE GREATEST ADVENTURES IN THE WORLD

TONY BRADMAN & TONY ROSS